"I felt the author did a great job pulling the reader into the story. I felt like I was actually *in* the story."
–Patti Pierce, author of *Truth and Grace Homeschool Academy* blog

"...a fun read which kept us turning pages, imagining what it may have been like during Noah's time and remembering that things change, but God doesn't, and we should always be thankful. I would definitely recommend the story to those looking for clean reading for kids and biblical fiction!"
–Martianne Stanger, author of *Training Happy Hearts* blog

"This one is a page-turner. Once you start, you won't want to put it down. The writing fills your imagination with vivid imagery. One thing that was fun for us to discuss, after everyone had a turn with the book, was how the [story] aligned with the Bible."
–Crystal Heft, author of *Living Abundantly* blog

"...a great book and we loved reading it aloud together! I recommend you grabbing a copy for your own family to read!"
–Felicia Mollohan, author of *Homeschool4Life* blog

IMAGINE

The Giant's Fall

Matt
Koceich

BARBOUR BOOKS

An Imprint of Barbour Publishing, Inc.

© 2019 by Matt Koceich

Print ISBN 978-1-68322-944-5

eBook Editions:
Adobe Digital Edition (.epub) 978-1-64352-123-7
Kindle and MobiPocket Edition (.prc) 978-1-64352-124-4

Published by Barbour Books, an imprint of Barbour Publishing, Inc., 1810 Barbour Drive, Uhrichsville, Ohio 44683, www.barbourbooks.com

Our mission is to inspire the world with the life-changing message of the Bible.

ecpa Member of the
Evangelical Christian
Publishers Association

Printed in the United States of America.
06496   0419   BP

THOUSANDS OF YEARS AGO

The giant grabbed the girl and lifted her high into the air. He yanked her up so hard and fast she thought she was going to pass out. Her struggle to get out of the monster's powerful grip was over. Despite the way the Bible story ended, it appeared the girl was not going to be as lucky as the young shepherd boy.

Ten-year-old Wren Evans enjoyed the feeling of victory. She had come face-to-face with the gargantuan man they called Goliath. She had survived his presence once before, but now her luck had run out.

She writhed in his powerful grip like a snake, trying to break free. It was no use. She was just a fourth-grader, and he was a nine-foot-tall superhuman.

The giant squeezed his fist and slowly pushed the air from Wren's lungs.

As she hung there, high above the plain, her life began to slip away. . . .

CHAPTER 1

"With man this is impossible, but with God all things are possible."

"Matthew nineteen twenty-one," Wren said as she looked at the index card in her hand. She turned to stare out the school bus window, lost in thought. She saw a black-and-white cow with its head up, like it was trying to say hi to her.

"Twenty-six."

"What?" She was still distracted by the Chick-fil-A cow that stared at her from the field.

"Twenty-six. You said twenty-one, but the verse is nineteen twenty-*six*."

"Beth, look at that cow. Not a care in the world. No school. *Nothing*."

"Wren, you want to be a cow? Really?"

Beth was a great friend. She was always good for a laugh to ease the stress.

"No, I don't want to be a cow. I just wish things were different."

The light turned green, and the school bus chugged forward. Wren watched the cow go back to eating grass. She looked down at the Bible verse her mother had written on the neon-green index card. It had been her mother's favorite verse. She had prayed it over her baby girl every morning before she left for her teaching job at the elementary school.

Wren asked Beth the next question. "Can you come over later and look at the book before I mail it off?"

They had been working on a kids' picture book about a girl who loses her mother to cancer. The book was written to honor Wren's mom who had passed away from cancer only a year ago. The girls planned to give any money they earned to cancer research. Their teacher had a friend who worked for a publishing house and agreed to print the book.

"Of course," Beth said. "My brother doesn't have baseball tonight. I'll ask my mom for a ride."

"Okay. Just text me." Wren kept her eyes on the index card. It was the only piece of her mother she had left that really meant something. There were the pictures and the memories, but the index card was the thing that gave her hope.

The bus traveled on down the country road, navigating the curves and straightaways all the same: slow. The beauty of nature was erased by Wren's impatience. All she wanted to do was get home and look at the book draft one last time. It was homemade, nothing but the printed pages glued to construction paper along with their hand-drawn pictures, but it felt like the real deal.

Her father promised they would get it to the post office before the five o'clock pickup. That way the publisher could have it by the beginning of next week.

Added to the slowness of the bus was the silence that hung over the students. Normally, the ride home was a cacophony of noises: shouts, laughs, whispers, coughs, sneezes, singing. Now all Wren could hear was the buzzing of the big bus tires rolling over Highway 15. Even Lucy Jones was quiet. And that girl could talk.

Suddenly sirens tore through the quiet, ripping it to shreds. Just as the bus crossed over Dog Creek, Wren saw the red lights. The bus pulled over. A fire engine pulled out onto the road in front of them and drove north. Seconds later, a police SUV zoomed past with its lights flashing and siren wailing, warning drivers to get out of the way.

The bus resumed its mission of delivering the children of Jobe Elementary to their respective houses. Wren still stared at the card. Oh, how she wished her mother would be home to greet her.

"I see smoke! Look!"

The voice belonged to Allen Decker, the obnoxious class clown. He sat in the front seat by the main bus door. Wren saw that Allen was looking through the huge windshield, his neck craned to get a good view.

"Wow! Whatever's burning is *toast*!" Allen added the last word for effect, as if something burning wasn't enough drama.

She couldn't see anything from her seat.

And just like that, the silence was erased. The bus erupted in nervous chatter as the children offered a hundred thousand guesses about what was burning.

As the bus crawled to a halt, Wren noticed they weren't at a regular stop. She got up and leaned over the seats directly across the aisle and saw why the bus had stopped. Her entire street had been blocked off by emergency vehicles. She thought she saw her dad standing in the middle of the street, surrounded by rescue personnel.

"Let me out!" Wren hustled up the aisle toward the front of the bus.

The driver had the door open for her. "Be careful."

But Wren wasn't listening. She was already running down Southcrest Drive.

Once her eyes scanned the street and her brain caught up and realized it was her house that was burning, her legs seemed to slow down. It was like her feet had gone from concrete to quicksand. She willed herself forward to where her dad was standing. When she got to him, his arms opened to receive her in a bear hug.

"I'm sorry, honey! I'm so sorry!"

"What happened?" The question was out of Wren's

mouth before she could take it back.

"I don't know. I was out back on a phone call. When I came in, I smelled something burning. It was the TV wire in my bedroom. By the time I got in there, the curtains were burning. I tried to put it out, but it spread too fast."

Wren looked at the black shell of her house. The destroyed structure stood there like a charcoal skeleton. Three firefighters were holding the firehose and shooting water over it. This could *not* be happening.

Her book manuscript!

"Dad, the box on my desk. Did you grab it?"

"I'm sorry, angel. I grabbed our laptops. The firefighters came and pulled me out. Oh baby, I'm so sorry!" He grabbed Wren in another hug.

But the nightmare kept getting worse. Wren couldn't do this anymore. Her life was a dead end. Impossible to overcome. It felt like God had simply walked away and let her and her dad fend for themselves.

She pulled away from her father's embrace and took off running. If her lungs and heart could handle it, she'd run forever and never stop.

She ran down the street.

Away from the fire.

Away from her dad.

Away from the pain.

When her legs and lungs finally protested, she collapsed on the sidewalk. She put her face to her knees. The green index card was still in her hand.

"Open her eyes."

The voice belonged to a woman, but when Wren looked around, no one was there.

She must be losing her mind. The fire was the last straw. Why would God allow this? It was too much for anyone to bear, let alone a young kid.

The world was broken.

Gone.

Wren closed her eyes and prayed that when she opened them again, she'd be staring at her phone and the alarm to get up for school would be ringing. And this whole wicked day would never have happened.

She cried out to God, "Why did You forget me my dad? Why?" Her body shook from the stress of She clenched her fists and tried to hold back a nev of tears. It was just too much.

Way too much.

She rubbed her face and wished more than any-thing that this whole day—whole life, really—was just a bad dream she'd wake up from any second now. She wished she could see her mother one more time. Just one more hug. . .

But she wasn't in a dream. And her mother wasn't here to give her a comforting hug.

CHAPTER 2

1020 B.C.

BETHLEHEM

Wren opened her eyes.

Panic set in as she saw an utterly different landscape than her street. Wherever she was, it certainly wasn't Kansas. She stood and turned in a complete circle, hoping to see the woman who had said something about opening someone's eyes.

What happened? Where am I?

She looked around and couldn't see anything that resembled her home. She was in the middle of a beautiful green pasture!

No. No. No.

What just happened?

"Where am I?" Wren asked the new world around her.

She took in more of the landscape. She was standing on one side of a large valley. Where the pasture stopped, a massive field of grain grew. It looked like all the wheat she saw back home. Her grandfather grew wheat on his farm and loved to tell her random facts about it. Like Kansas produces the most wheat in the United States, and all the wheat grown there in one year would fill train cars that stretched from western Kansas all the way to the Atlantic Ocean.

She was still holding her mother's neon-green index card.

"With man this is impossible, but with God all things are possible."

Reading the verse again gave her a boost of confidence. She had to figure out what was going on. When she looked to the right—where her neighborhood should be—Wren saw a herd of sheep grazing. There were at least thirty of the fluffy white animals roaming around. Petting the creatures would surely help ease the stress of her day.

She blinked a few more times and shook her head. Her mind had to be playing tricks on her from the drama of the day. But the sheep were still grazing, and there was no concrete, no houses, and no Kansas around for miles.

I'll pet the sheep and calm down. That's the plan. Pet the cute sheep and calm down!

Wren slowly walked up to the closest sheep and stuck her hand out. She always did that with her friend's dog so it could sniff her first. Did sheep follow the same rules?

The sheep licked her hand instead of sniffing it. Its tongue felt like sandpaper. It tickled and made her laugh. She kneeled down and rubbed the serene animal behind the ears. The other sheep were curious and started to come closer to her.

Wherever she was, it was more relaxing than the real world of Mulvane, Kansas. Maybe this was heaven. Maybe her very young heart had finally had enough of all the stress and simply stopped beating. But if this was heaven, where were all the people?

Wren welcomed the sheep as they surrounded her. It

felt good to be here. No sadness. Just beautiful sunlight. Clear blue sky. Endless green prairie that stretched to the horizon.

The adorable sheep.

She needed to find her dad and bring him here too.

She absorbed the beauty of the moment.

But just like back home, all beautiful things had to end.

When she looked up from petting the sheep, she couldn't believe what she saw. A brown bear stood on the crest of a nearby hill. The huge creature had to weigh more than three grown men! The bear looked at her and swung its big fuzzy head back and forth.

The bear began walking down the hillside in her direction. Its massive legs worked like a machine to push the lumbering giant forward.

After a few paces, the bear had built up momentum and began running. Wren figured she looked appetizing to the bear and didn't want to imagine what would happen when it finally caught up to her. She immediately thought of her Uncle Nick.

He had a cat named Bandit, and when Wren was

little she loved playing with him. She would get rough with the cat, and her uncle would say, "Careful. If you keep playing with Bandit like that, there'll be nothing left of you except your hair, teeth, and eyeballs."

If bears could talk, the one coming after her would surely be quoting Uncle Nick.

She looked around the pasture. There was a huge boulder sitting about a football field's length away.

She had no choice. Wren had to make a run for it. She was a sitting duck where she was, and today she didn't feel like getting eaten by a bear.

She jumped to her feet and ran as fast as she could to the boulder. She prayed she didn't trip over anything, because if she did, that would be the end of it.

As she ran, she could hear the bear grunting. The sound got louder as the humongous animal got closer. She looked over her shoulder and saw that the bear was so close. She guessed only twenty yards behind!

Wren thanked the Lord she had done gymnastics for the last five years. She decided that she was going to do a killer vault up onto the rock and escape her attacker.

But the bear had different plans. It closed the gap on

its human prey. Only fifteen yards behind. . .like a runaway train barreling down the tracks.

Lord, please help me get to the rock!

Wren pushed harder. She concentrated on pumping her legs up and down, as fast as she could get them to move.

The bear closed the distance between them. Only ten yards behind. . .

Lord, please get me to the rock!

So close now. But then a sharp, stabbing pain shot up her right leg, from her ankle all the way up to her hip. It interrupted her stride. Her right leg buckled, causing her to slow down.

The animal's grunting grew louder. It sounded like a boat motor, gurgling and churning in the water.

Only five yards behind.

This was it.

Wren took a deep breath and used every ounce of strength she could muster—and jumped.

She made it without falling and executed her best vault yet, landing almost near the top of the massive stone. The bear's claws raked against the boulder, and a disappointed roar came from its hungry mouth. It stood on its hind legs, and with its left paw on the boulder, swatted at her with its right.

The bear kept clawing while she prayed he would forget he was hungry or get distracted by something else.

Minutes passed, and the bear eventually lost interest. He dropped to all four paws and turned back to the pasture. She realized that her prayer was being answered. The bear had his sights set on a new meal: the sheep.

There was nothing she could do. She couldn't run after the bear and make it go away.

She watched in utter helplessness as the bear trotted up to one of the peaceful creatures. Wren couldn't look. She shut her eyes and covered her ears.

After a minute, she opened her eyes and put her hands down. That's when she saw a young man standing between her and the flock. He couldn't have been more than sixteen but had biceps that would make her gymnastics coach proud.

His outfit was strange. He wore something that looked like a leather vest and baggy tan pants that stopped way above his ankles. Did the boy not know about the bear behind him?

He held a big wooden stick in his right hand. The top of the stick was shaped in the form of a big hook.

He looked at her and waved. She was too frightened to wave back. Instead, she pointed past him and hoped he would turn around in time to see the mammoth predator.

Instead he waved at her again then turned around to see what she was pointing at.

And then he did what Wren would have never guessed he would do. The young man took off running into the forest after the bear!

She waited at the rock and watched the remaining sheep mill around in a tight huddle.

A few minutes later, she watched the young man come back out of the forest holding the sheep! He had blood on his arms and legs, but he seemed to be walking just fine. He came back and put the rescued sheep down with its friends.

Who could fight a bear and win?

CHAPTER 3

Wren didn't have long to think about that question, because at that same moment an actual lion came out of the woods.

She couldn't believe it. Where on earth was she?

The lion didn't have a mane, so she guessed it was a girl cat. She thought she'd read somewhere in one of her science books that the girl lions were the ones who hunted.

Girl power!

She would have laughed at her own joke, but given the situation, nothing was funny.

It looked like the lion had come after the same thing the bear had. The massive cat moved slowly toward the sheep, its large brown eyes locked on its target.

The worst part of all this was that Wren felt helpless sitting there on the rock. The poor sheep couldn't catch a break. First the bear. . .

The lion charged at the closest sheep and snatched it up in its fangs.

The predator took its prey into the forest, and once again, the young man ran after the sheep, staff in hand.

There was no way on earth he could beat the bear *and* the lion.

But that's exactly what he did. Covered in more blood than before, he reappeared from the woods a few minutes later holding the sheep in his bloody arms!

No way.

Wren could not believe what she had just witnessed. Part of her was afraid to say anything to the boy in fear he might attack her like he did the two wild animals. But then she remembered how he had waved to her earlier. Plus, she thought of how bad life had gotten back in Kansas. She was more eager than afraid to meet this young man.

I've got nothing to lose!

She stood up on the boulder with her hands in the air.

Don't attack me like you did the bear and the lion!

"Hello! I'm Wren. What's your name?"

"I'm David."

David? Why does all this seem familiar?

"How on earth did you do that?"

"Do what?"

Wren laughed. "You fought a bear and a lion and saved the sheep. How did you do that?"

"Well, Wren. . ." The young man paused to pick up one of the other sheep. "I had help."

"I didn't see anybody."

"God helped me. He's invisible. That's why you couldn't see Him."

Sheep.

A bear.

A lion.

David.

God.

She put it all together.

"Are you David from the Bible?"

"From the what?"

"The Bible."

David looked at her and considered her words. "I'm not familiar with this Bible you mention. But, like I said, the Lord is my shepherd. He helps me through every problem. When the bear and lion came for my flock, I knew that God would give me the courage to protect what He has entrusted to me. He is my rod and my staff."

"Yes! You're David from the Bible! You said those exact words about God being your shepherd in Psalm twenty-three." Wren sat on her bottom and slid down off the boulder. "I can't believe this! How is this possible?"

"I'm sorry. I don't understand what you're talking about."

How did I get back to Bible times?

Where did Kansas go?

"David, have you heard of a place called Kansas?"

The young shepherd shook his head.

Wren thought about the Bible story. "Are we in Bethlehem?"

David's eyes grew wide. "Yes."

How on earth is this happening?

"I'm from a place called Kansas. It's a state in the United States. I don't know how I got here, but this is so cool. Getting to meet you is awesome!"

"I'm glad to meet you too, Wren. Your clothes are. . .not like mine."

She looked down at her outfit. Of course, what she had on would seem crazy to David. A lot of time had passed between this Bible story and 2019!

"Yeah, I guess you're right. But how did you do it?"

"Do what?" David asked.

"The bear and the lion. How did you save the sheep?"

The young man didn't hesitate. "The Lord rescued me. I didn't doubt that He would, so I ran after the bear. If I doubted God was with me, it would do me no good, and the sheep would have perished."

Wren stared at David like he was some superhero from one of the gazillion Marvel movies. His confidence, given the stress of the situation, was insane. "How did you get the sheep away from the bear and lion? I'd think they'd drop the sheep and eat you instead."

"When I went after the bear, I struck it on the side with my staff. When it turned on me, I shoved my hand in its mouth and pulled on its tongue so hard I thought it would rip right out of its mouth. I did the same thing with the lion."

She couldn't believe what she was hearing.

"And that's how I got the sheep out of their mouths. But I must hurry. My father asked me to take provisions to my brothers who are with the Israelite army. Will you come with me?"

Wren didn't have to think about that question.

"Sure!"

CHAPTER 4

"Do you have everything, son?"

Wren stood next to David's father, Jesse, and watched the young man finish arranging the supplies on a large piece of fabric that looked like a very uncomfortable bedsheet.

"Yes, Father."

Jesse regarded his son's work. "Tell me what you have, so we can be sure."

"Yes, Father. I packed the ephah of roasted grain and ten loaves of bread for my brothers. I also gathered these ten cheeses for their commander. Anything else?"

The older man considered his son's question. "No, that should be all. Remember, please ask how they are doing, and come back quickly with an update. By the

Father's grace, I pray they are all okay."

David gathered the four corners of the sheet and pulled up, keeping the supplies from falling out. He lifted the whole makeshift backpack over his shoulder and set out toward the field where the sheep were still grazing.

"Come on, Wren. I need to have the shepherd next door watch my flock while we are away."

Her mind was still blown. How was it possible that she could be in this amazing place with the great Bible character David? She didn't have time to think about it, because David had already set off toward the field where she had first met him.

She looked at David and still couldn't believe that someone his size could fight against those two powerful wild animals. How could that be? None of this made sense, but she'd witnessed him saving the sheep, not once but *twice*! She shook her head and caught up to him.

Wren saw an older man holding a wooden staff, standing in the middle of the path. He smiled when he saw David.

"Ah, my friend. What can I do for you?"

"Reuben, this is my friend Wren."

"Hello, *Wren*. That's a beautiful name I've never heard before."

She smiled. "My mother loved birds."

The old shepherd smiled.

David put his sack of supplies down on the ground in front of his feet. "I need your help watching my flock while I take these supplies to my brothers."

"No worries," said Reuben. "How is your father?"

"He's fine."

The old shepherd nodded. "Go. Your sheep are safe with me."

"Thank you." David gathered the corners of the sheet and lifted it up over his shoulder again. He set off down the path. Wren followed.

Every now and then she checked her watch out of habit.

"What is that on your arm?" David asked.

"It's called a watch."

"A watch?"

"Yes. It tells me what time it is."

David looked confused. "Wren, I haven't heard that

31

thing talk. Yet, you say it tells you something. I don't understand."

"It's a figure of speech. The watch doesn't really talk."

David kept his eyes on the path and a tight grip on the supply sack. "What's a figure of speech?"

She chuckled and thought about the best way to explain the concept. David interrupted her.

"Please tell me later. We've arrived. This is Sokoh."

The path led to the top of a very wide hill. In front of them, the grass-covered land descended into a massive bowl-shaped valley. On either end of the bowl, on her right and on her left, hundreds of men in various forms of armor were huddled together, moving around in random patterns. Wren thought it looked like the result of two human-sized ant piles that had been disturbed. She could hear the men yelling as they moved.

"The voices are shouting the war cry. We must hurry!"

David started jogging toward one end of the valley, and Wren followed on his heels.

As they got closer, she felt the intensity in the air.

"To your battle positions!"

She had gone from a peaceful pasture filled with

sheep to the middle of a battlefield filled with hundreds of soldiers carrying scary swords.

When they reached the camp, David worked his way through the sea of armed men, waving a greeting to some and ignoring others. Wren stayed as close to him as physically possible.

After a while, he stopped in front of a man who looked frazzled, with gray hair sticking out in every direction and a weathered face covered in wrinkles.

David handed his bedsheet backpack to the man.

"Wren, this is Malec, keeper of supplies for the Israelite army."

Wren put a hand out to greet the man, but he ignored her and started going through the food that David had carried all the way from Bethlehem.

"The bread and grain are for my brothers, the sons of Jesse. The cheese is for the commander." David didn't wait for a reply. "Come on, Wren. Let's find my brothers!"

He ran out to the battle lines, and she followed, secretly wishing she didn't have to experience this part of the Bible story. But as soon as she felt the fear, a new thought entered her mind that took away most of the worry. She knew how this story ended! She chuckled again, glad that David wasn't looking. He might think she was weird.

Wren saw her new friend stop in front of a young man who was much taller than David. He was very muscular and had long brown hair. The two talked for a minute before David walked away and threaded a path through the crowd of soldiers.

"WHY DO YOU COME OUT AND LINE UP FOR BATTLE?"

The voice sounded like it was coming out of speakers at a rock concert rather than one man's mouth. She jumped and turned to see where the voice came from. Her brain couldn't process what her eyes saw. A super giant soldier stood on the opposite side of the valley, glaring at her and the Israelites.

The soldiers closest to Wren began running. Not toward the giant, but away from him. Their eyes were wide with fear.

"That's the giant from Gath!" one of the men yelled as he ran past.

"Is that Goliath?" She shouted the question to be

heard over the scurrying of troops.

"Yes," one of the soldiers said. "The man is over nine feet tall!"

Wren couldn't believe that a human could be that massive. Bigger than Hulk. More intimidating than Thor. He had a bronze helmet on his enormous head and a coat of gigantic bronze fish scales around his chest and stomach.

A different soldier standing nearby offered another observation about the superhuman. "The word around camp is that his armor weighs over a hundred pounds!"

"AM I NOT A PHILISTINE, AND ARE YOU NOT THE SERVANTS OF SAUL?"

She also noticed the giant wore bronze armor that covered his legs, from his knees down to his ankles. He had a bronze javelin slung on his back, the same way that Captain America wore his circular patriotic shield. Wren figured that was to throw at someone running at him, but who on earth would want to run toward that guy?

Wren saw David walking back to her, a new soldier at his side.

"Wren, this is my oldest brother, Eliab. Eliab this is

my new friend, Wren."

Eliab pointed back to the giant. "That creature of a man points his long wooden spear at us as he issues his taunts, morning and night. Our men figure that the huge iron point at its tip must weigh a hefty amount. He's been at it for forty days now!"

"CHOOSE A MAN, AND HAVE HIM COME DOWN TO ME. IF HE IS ABLE TO FIGHT AND KILL ME, WE WILL BECOME YOUR SUBJECTS."

The giant's voice was so loud and powerful, the ground shook. The Israelites retreated like a buffalo stampede. Wren felt like she was standing in the middle of a big earthquake. How could anyone beat that guy in a fight? Impossible. But, again, she remembered how all of this ended and wasn't as afraid as she would have been.

"IF I OVERCOME HIM, YOU WILL BECOME OUR SUBJECTS AND SERVE US."

Some of the soldiers who hadn't retreated gathered around them. One spoke directly to David. "The giant is a problem that won't go away. There is no solution. Despite the size and will of our people, Goliath is the one thing we cannot overcome."

Wren watched David as he stared at the giant from Gath. The young shepherd had a confident look on his face that was different than the apprehensive looks on the Israelites' faces.

"This giant is a disgrace!" David shouted. "Who is this Philistine that he should defy the armies of the living God?"

Eliab grabbed his little brother's arm and yanked him around so that the two siblings were face-to-face. She was confused. Why would David's brother do that?

The roar of the Philistine army rose up around the giant. They cheered on their champion and mighty warrior.

Why would the Israelites run away and fear this giant? If they had God on their side, why would they ever worry about this superhuman. . .or anything else for that matter?

The same reason you feel like God didn't do anything to keep your sweet mother from passing away. The same reason you feel like a God who really cared wouldn't let your house burn down. The same reason you feel like a God who is supposed to love His children would have kept your manuscript from being destroyed in the flames.

She shut her eyes and hoped that when she opened them again, all this Bible story stuff would be nothing more than a dream.

CHAPTER 5

But it didn't go away.

It was all still right there in front of her when she opened her eyes. The giant still taunted the Israelites, and the Israelites still trembled in fear. Wren saw David was still talking to his brother.

"Why have you come down here? Only to watch the battle?" It seemed like Eliab's anger had boiled up inside him as he spewed out his words. "You are so conceited!"

David shook his head and held his hands out. "Now what have I done? Can't I even speak?"

She felt a little awkward because she wasn't sure what she should do. Walk around and meet people? Introduce herself?

She didn't wonder for long, because a lady dressed in a red shirt and jeans came out of the crowd of soldiers. Her clothing style didn't match the others. She dressed like Wren dressed.

"Hey, over here!"

The lady heard Wren call her and headed over to where she was standing.

"Hello, I'm Josephine."

Wren scanned her memory files and couldn't remember a lady named Josephine in the David and Goliath story.

"Hello. I'm Wren."

The lady looked at her and shook her head. "You're not from here."

"I'm from Kansas. And you don't look like you're from around here either."

Josephine smiled. "No, I'm not from this place."

"Do you know where Kansas is?"

"Yes, child. And I also know *when* you're from. But there isn't time for explanations. I need to show you some things that will help you on your journey."

Wren was confused. "Journey?"

"Right now, I don't want you to ask questions. Right now, I just want you to have faith. Okay?"

Strangely, Wren felt a peace in Josephine's presence. "Okay."

"Good. Now follow me."

She followed the lady back through the crowd of retreating soldiers out into an open area of grass. Josephine led her right into the middle of the valley. From her new vantage point, Wren looked up and saw the two hills on either side of her. Both armies were in motion. However, like moving water in a cup, neither moved too far. Just back and forth, back and forth, over the close confines of their respective hills.

The giant stood tall, towering over all of man and nature.

Josephine pointed in his direction.

"Now, I'm going to show you something, but I promise you have nothing to be afraid of. Okay?"

Wren didn't know what was coming next, but ever since landing back in the Bible story of David and Goliath, she had decided to soak in as much as she could. Besides, she didn't get a bad vibe from Josephine. "Okay."

"Good. Now close your eyes and count to three."

Wren looked at the lady.

"Go on. Close your eyes and count to three. After you get to three, open them. Just don't panic when you do. I promise I'm here to watch over you." Josephine put a hand on Wren's shoulder.

"Okay, here goes." She closed her eyes. "One. . . two. . .three."

"Open her eyes," Josephine said.

Wren couldn't imagine who she was speaking to. But then, she opened her eyes and the whole world shifted. Her brain was flooded with images she had never seen before.

She was standing on sand, and a great wind had begun to blow around her. She looked at Josephine and felt her mouth drop open, wider than her eyes had gone. The lady was glowing, and her red shirt and jeans were gone. Wren thought she might be wearing a white shirt and pants, but she really couldn't tell for sure because of all the light that was radiating *from* Josephine.

And wings?

Yes! Josephine had wings with white feathers!

"What's happening?"

"Don't worry, child. As I said, you have nothing to fear. You are safe here." The lady moved her wings ever so slightly.

Nothing she had ever felt in her short life compared to what Wren was feeling now. It wasn't fear like being scared of bad things. She was in awe of what her eyes saw. Past Josephine, out across the valley, a dark cloud swirled. As she watched, the cloud broke up into pieces. Wisps of black smoke-like bands moved in random patterns of flight over the valley.

Apparently sensing Wren's apprehension, Josephine stretched out a wing. "Hold on to me!"

Wren grabbed the wing.

The black bands slowly morphed into shapes—the shapes of men—and all landed on the valley floor around them. She squeezed Josephine's wing tighter. Josephine turned so that her back was facing Wren.

"Get on!"

Get on?

Wren let go of the wing and grabbed on to the lady's shoulders. Both wings shot out and pushed down, lifting her and Josephine up into the air.

I'm flying!

Unbelievable!

"What's going on?" Wren shouted over the rushing wind. The valley looked smaller and smaller the higher Josephine flew. Cold air rushed across her face, blowing her ponytail around like a pinwheel.

"Hold on!" Josephine kept her wings stretched wide as she banked to the right.

Wren looked in that direction and noticed they were almost directly over the Philistine army.

Josephine pumped her wings two more times, and they flew out past them. Wren looked down and saw the dark shapes on the ground were moving toward the Israelites. But then one of the figures turned and walked in the opposite direction toward the Philistines. This dark shape was much larger than all the others.

Josephine adjusted her direction to follow the track of the large one. "That's Ra'zeil. He's a leader of the enemy's army!"

Wren watched as the shape in question swirled around the giant named Goliath. After a few swirls, the dark moving cloud morphed into a dark giant the same size as the superhuman from Gath. Josephine pumped her majestic white wings a few more times and changed her course so they could watch the two giants.

"What are you?" Wren asked her.

"An angel!"

An angel? "Awesome!"

But her excitement of flying with an angel was quickly erased.

She looked down and saw the dark figure engulf Goliath completely. Simultaneously, the dark shapes that had been marching toward David and his brothers stopped. They all turned and faced her. She looked down and could see the figures all had purple eyes.

In unison, all the dark shapes out on the valley shot up, off the ground, and flew right at Wren.

CHAPTER 6

They came fast, like black missiles set out to destroy her.

"HOLD ON!"

Josephine darted to the left, and Wren held on with every ounce of strength she had in her. The darkness shot past them, missing them by inches.

"I'm going to set you down on that cliff. There's a man there who will help you. Stay with him until I return, and don't be afraid!"

Josephine banked again and flew in the direction of a steep rocky formation. Wren looked back and saw the black mass change direction and resume its pursuit of her and Josephine. She still couldn't believe what was happening. She wanted to find her dad but didn't think he was in this place. She had no idea how to get back to him. For now, survival was the most pressing issue on the agenda.

Josephine corrected her flying course one last time and headed for a wide ledge that protruded from the cliff face. She took Wren there and set her down safely, all the while keeping an eye out for their enemy.

"I will come back for you. When you're ready, start climbing. Soon you will find my friend. Be brave!"

And just as quickly as they had landed, Josephine took off into the wide blue sky.

Wren looked up and saw the task ahead of her. The cliff face reminded her of the rock-climbing wall at camp last year. Hating heights with a passion, she'd refused to participate even though her friends begged her to do it. She still said no to the rock wall after several kids called her a chicken.

Now here she was, thousands of years away from camp and her friends, and anyone else for that matter. What was the point of all this? How did she get here?

The answers would have to wait because of the dark form that began to take shape in front of her. The shadows moved and swam around to make the outline of an adult. It had to be one of the smoke creatures that Wren saw coming up from the valley.

She turned and started to scale the side of the cliff.

"I'm not here to hurt you." The words came from the shadow below her. She ignored the thing and kept climbing up the wall.

"Your little picture book will sell a few copies to your friends and family, but that's it."

How did this *thing* know about the book? Wren found another ledge and pulled herself up on it. She sat with her back against the rock.

"Face it, you've got nothing. Nothing."

She started to argue with the creature but decided saying nothing was the best defense. It couldn't be human. The thing somehow knew about her.

"You don't have to say anything. That's okay. I know you. Your mother passed away from cancer, and your father is checked out. Your house burned down and took your little picture book with it. I'd say all of that combined means you truly have nothing."

How does this thing *know about that stuff?*

Wren kept her eyes on the creature and her mouth closed.

"I came here to offer you something better than all of the pain and loss you've been given."

The sound of the thing's voice was calm and inviting. Part of Wren wanted to speak now. She was interested in the offer of anything that didn't involve cancer, dying, or loss.

"Leave her alone, Ra'zeil!"

This new voice came from above her. She looked up and saw an older man who had long brown hair that reached his shoulders and a beard that looked like it had been growing unchecked for years.

"Mark Grant. You do have a way of annoying me. Please don't interrupt. I'm almost finished." The one named Ra'zeil inched closer to Wren, while the man named Mark began repelling down the cliff to join them.

She was trapped between the dark shadow man and the new man named Mark. Wren wondered if he was the friend Josephine mentioned earlier.

Ra'zeil kept climbing. "Wren, how would you like to help me?"

Mark Grant jumped down and joined her. "Don't

listen to him. He's a liar. They all are."

Now the dark one was a foot away from her. His body swirled like a hurricane trapped beneath an invisible layer of skin. Dark smoke churning in the places where a person's body would be. "Wren, you deserve to be done with all the yucky stuff. Let me show you a different way."

The last word wasn't fully out of the shadow man's mouth when the one named Mark ran at him. "Leave the girl alone!" He put his head down and rammed into the shadow's middle. The force carried both men to the edge of the cliff.

"Wren, go! Start climbing."

She was mesmerized by what she was witnessing. It looked like the two men were about to go over the side.

"Climb!" Mark yelled back to her while he wrestled the shadow man.

Wren hesitated.

"Now, before it's too late!" Mark continued his fight against the darkness.

She shook her head and went for it. She used her right hand to grab hold of a rock and pulled up. She took her left hand and used it to grab a new rock higher than the first. A gust of wind threatened her grip, but Wren held on. The only mistake she made was when she looked down to see the struggle between Mark and Ra'zeil. It broke her rhythm and she lost her momentum.

She was stuck halfway between where she had started and the ledge that Mark had come down from. Wren couldn't hold on. Her strength was slipping away, just like her hands from the rocks.

The sounds of the struggle continued below her.

Her left hand slipped off first.

Her body dropped and slammed against the rocky cliff. Hanging by her right hand was harder than anything she had ever done in her life.

And then she couldn't hang on any longer. The last ounce of fight she had left in her disappeared. Her right hand opened, and Wren's body gave in to the gravity that had been trying to yank her off the cliff.

She fell and shut her eyes. . .

. . .waiting for the ground to take her away.

CHAPTER 7

She closed her eyes and waited for the impact.

But her body landed in outstretched arms.

She looked up and saw that the person who had caught her was the same young man who had wrestled the lion and the bear.

"David!"

He set Wren down, and she shook her head. "I thought that was it."

"You thought what was what?"

Wren smiled. "I meant that I thought I was going to die."

"Oh, no, child. It's not your time. There's a lot of kingdom work to do. We need to hurry. We don't have much time. Let's go."

Wren followed David over a rocky path that went around the cliff. After a short amount of walking, they reached a cave.

"Do you know those two people who were fighting?" Wren was still a bit freaked out about the shadow man.

"What two people?"

"You didn't see a dark-cloud-looking dude and another man over there? They started wrestling."

"No. I got distracted back at camp arguing with my brother. When I went to look for you, you were gone. Someone told me to try here on the mountain. That's when I saw you trying to climb."

How could he not see them?

"Can we go back to the camp?" Wren didn't like the looks of the dark cave.

"Yes. But first I need to show you something. Plus, the Philistines sent troops to patrol this mountain. If we return now, we will surely be caught."

Wren followed David into the cave, surprised that enough natural light was present to make her able to see where they were.

"Here." David sat on the ground near a large stone.

Next to the stone was an object that resembled a small leather journal.

"This is a weird scroll of some kind. It has drawings of people that dress like you do." David handed the book to Wren.

She opened it and was shocked to see drawings of people, young and old, who were dressed in clothes from her time.

One drawing startled her, and she dropped the book onto the cave floor. David bent down to pick it up. "What?" He looked at her with a puzzled expression etched on his face.

"This picture here." She turned the pages and pointed to the drawing. "This is my mom!"

"Your mother? That is very odd. Maybe it just looks like your mom."

Suddenly, two Philistine soldiers appeared in the cave's entrance, each bearing an ominous silver sword.

And behind them stood the shadow man.

CHAPTER 8

"Don't move!"

They were trapped. The shadow man slipped around the soldiers and entered the cave.

"Go," David told Wren. He stepped forward to intercept the newcomers.

She had no choice but to turn and head deeper into the darkness. She couldn't see a thing, so she stretched her arms out in front of her.

She bumped into walls and only managed to move a few feet before the entire cave lit up like the morning sun had risen inside the stone walls. In reaction, Wren's eyes slammed shut.

"Don't move!"

She felt a hand clamp down on her arm. The hand

belonged to one of the soldiers. She saw that the other soldier had David.

What is the point of all this?

Why am I here?

None of this makes sense!

"Bring them back to the camp. Keep watch until Goliath can deal with the girl," the shadow man said.

She didn't understand what all this meant. The soldier pulled her out of the cave. She saw David being led away by the other soldier.

The soldiers led them down a path that made its way to the bottom of the hill. The whole time they walked, Wren kept looking for the shadow man. He never came out of the cave.

When they reached the place where the dusty path gave way to the prairie, Wren could see the giant again. He was standing out in front of the Philistine army facing the Israelites. Hands raised like he had just crossed an imaginary finish line.

"THIS DAY I DEFY THE ARMIES OF ISRAEL! GIVE ME A MAN, AND LET US FIGHT EACH OTHER!"

The giant's voice sounded like it was being pumped through a siren. It was deep, loud, and scary. His words shot through the air and hit her ears like heavy rocks. Each one powerful in its own way.

This is why the Israelite soldiers are afraid!

God, please help me get out of this place!

The soldiers led them deep into the Philistine camp. Wren watched as David was shoved into a tent. Her soldier led her a little farther before pushing her into another tent.

Inside the tent, Wren sat on the ground and buried her face in her drawn-up knees. She could not figure out how or why she was trapped in this otherworld. At first, she thought it was cool to be able to experience a Bible story. But now, stuck in the enemy's camp, no part of this bizarre trip was fun. Wren felt just like she did when her mom passed away from the terrible cancer.

Being caught in the Philistine's camp made her stomach churn under the wave of nerves that crashed over her body. This was also just like when the school bus turned onto their street and she saw the fire trucks.

Overcome.

And just like with all those real-world problems of pain and loss, she had no answers here either.

"I understand. Believe me, I understand."

She heard the words. They were spoken aloud, but no one was with her in the tent.

"All things, Wren. . .all things are possible."

What's happening? I'm hearing voices that are not real. I'm hearing a man speak, but no one is in here with me.

"I'm here with you, Wren. Just believe."

The ground beneath her rumbled. The tent poles shook. She stood and nearly lost her balance but steadied herself before falling. She wanted to find the owner of the voice.

She peeked through the opening of the tent and saw the group of soldiers who had been guarding her. They all stepped back to let the giant pass by.

Goliath was back!

Each step he took toward the tent shook the ground harder the closer he came.

"WHERE IS SHE?"

Oh Lord, please keep me safe!

Wren looked around for a way out, but there were guards all around the outside of the tent. She could hear the soldiers telling the giant where she was being held.

And then the ground stopped quaking. And the loud siren voice stopped booming. And then came the silence.

But it was only the calm before the storm. The eye of the hurricane.

A massive hand pulled back the tent flap. Wren instinctively jumped back and pressed herself into the corner, holding down a scream so she wouldn't give away her position.

The giant's hand moved back and forth. Back and forth. Back and—

The huge hand found her.

"COME OUT!" Goliath screamed.

The hand grabbed her in a tight grip and pulled her out and up into daylight.

Staring into the eyes of the hideous giant man, Wren discovered a terrible new truth.

All things were *not* possible.

Goliath smiled.

Tightened his grip.

Her body couldn't do a thing against his power.

"Please, God! Help me!"

CHAPTER 9

Caught in the giant's clutches gave Wren a feeling of horror much worse than when the bus turned the corner and she realized it was her house that was burning. Back there, her father could buy a new house and solve the problem. Here, there was nothing she could do. A hopelessness so deep—she felt like she was drowning—smothered her soul.

God, please help me. Lord, make this stop!

She was confused, because this was not how the Bible story went. Why was this happening?

"YOU ARE JUST LIKE THOSE ISRAELITES!"

Goliath's words and foul breath washed over Wren in a sickening wave that crashed over her failing hope. It was bad enough that in the real world she had lost her mother, her house, and basically her father. But now, here in this otherworld, she was about to lose her life too.

Please, God! I can't do this anymore. It feels like You've left me alone. Please help me!

For some reason, at that exact moment, she was overcome by the thought of her mother. She remembered a story her mother had told about a butterfly. Thinking about the story always made her believe that God really *does* care.

ooooo

Wren's mother was a schoolteacher before the cancer came like a thief and took it all away. Rachel Evans taught fifth-graders how to read and write. Mostly she tried to get them excited about learning any chance she got. The school she worked at was smack-dab in the middle of a very low-income section of the city. The parents saw Mrs. Evans as a glorified day-care provider. Whatever she wanted to do with the students was fine by them. As long as she didn't call and ask for parent-teacher conferences.

It came before the cancer, in hindsight, an omen of sorts. But still it came.

The butterfly.

But before the butterfly, before the cancer, came a blessing named Larissa Willard. Larissa was a teaching assistant who worked with students with special needs. As the story went, Rachel knew of Larissa, but had never met the woman formally. In the four years they had worked in the same school building, Rachel remembered only one time she said hello to Larissa as the two passed in the hallway. Once. Looking back, Rachel was embarrassed to think she wasted all that time.

The following year, Rachel found out that Larissa would be in her classroom assisting a new student. The two ladies struck up a friendship, and Rachel wound up giving Larissa the nickname "Jazz." Larissa would always bring jazz CDs into the classroom for Rachel to play while the students were doing their daily writing assignment. Rachel quickly fell in love with the melodic sounds of Miles Davis, Thelonious Monk, Duke Ellington, and John Coltrane. The two ladies would laugh at all the stressful things that teaching brought, and they would cry at all the sadness that was thrown their way.

But through it all, Rachel sensed something very

different about Jazz. The lady was always talking about Jesus. And not in a preachy sort of way. Larissa talked about Jesus like they were next-door neighbors. She would be talking about how some crazy driver cut her off in traffic and made her blood boil, but then say something like, "You know, Rachel, Jesus was spit on and punched! Can you believe that? The man came to die for me, and the soldiers spit in His face and punched Him. Jesus took all of that for me! Mercy, sister. . .Jesus helped put my road rage into perspective. I sure do love Him."

At that time, Rachel didn't have Jesus in her heart and was curious about the faith Jazz showed. Over lunch, she'd started to ask Jazz questions about the Bible and her faith. Jazz, in return, quoted numerous Bible verses and even prayed for Rachel. And still, none of it came across as *weird*. For Rachel, listening to Jazz talk about Jesus actually filled her heart with joy.

And then life stepped in and gave Jazz some very bad news.

The doctors told her it was cancer. There was a tumor growing, and things didn't look promising. Rachel couldn't believe the news. How could this happen? That was the middle of November.

"Rachel, I'm sorry, but I can't work anymore. I told them I'm going to try and make it to Thanksgiving, but then I have to resign."

"Come on, Jazz. Don't apologize. You'll be fine." Rachel wasn't so sure.

Just a few weeks later, Thanksgiving break came, and Rachel watched her new friend suffer under the ravaging disease.

Things got so bad that on the last day on the job—a rainy Friday before Thanksgiving break—Larissa's daughter had to walk her to the car. Rachel would never forget standing at the school entrance watching her dear friend shuffle through the falling rain. She felt as if her heart was breaking.

Rachel was frustrated, because she liked to be in control of things. Everything in Jazz's life had come undone, and Rachel couldn't do a thing to stop the cancer.

What Rachel didn't know until later was that Larissa had left a page of Bible verses on Rachel's desk with a note on it. The note said for Rachel not to worry, because Jazz knew who her Great Physician was. Larissa also said that she hoped the verses would bless Rachel while the two were apart.

A month passed.

More rain fell, and more lessons were learned, but Rachel still wondered how God could be a part of Larissa's pain.

And then came Christmas.

Rachel received a call from Larissa. The doctors had not only removed all the cancer but gave her a clean bill of health. Jazz was going to come back to work after the New Year.

When Jazz returned, it was like a whole new person took over her body. Rachel couldn't believe how revitalized her friend looked and acted. It was nothing short of a miracle.

Rachel was ready.

For Jesus.

Right there in the classroom, while the students were at music class, Rachel held Larissa's hands and prayed for Jesus to come into her heart and take over. And then the craziest thing happened. A beautiful butterfly with yellow and black wings fluttered into the classroom and landed right on Rachel and Larissa's clasped hands. They stood there for what felt like an eternity, just staring at the gorgeous and delicate creature.

When the kids came back from music, Rachel let go of Larissa's hands, and the butterfly took flight.

ooooo

Exactly one year from that beautiful, life-changing experience, Wren's mother was diagnosed with an aggressive form of cancer.

Three months later she was gone.

At the cemetery, Wren was holding her father's hand as they listened to their pastor preach about God's love and strength in times of ultimate sadness. And then a yellow and black butterfly came and landed on their clasped hands.

That's when Wren knew that God cared about His children. And that no matter how bad things may be, God is good. And just like this butterfly, He sends signs to His loved ones so they will know they are never alone.

ooooo

The memory of the butterfly didn't make the giant go away, but it did help Wren keep her faith in God. The butterfly in both memories helped her have the courage to keep believing.

Goliath's mean face stared at her. She felt like a fly who was about to be swatted out of its misery.

She tried to wriggle free of the giant's grip, but it was pointless. His fingers were like a vise.

But, if Larissa Willard could trust God with the cancer, and her mother could trust God with her soul, Wren could trust God to deal with this impossible situation. Because God, in her mind, was indeed bigger than the giants.

CHAPTER 10

The giant held on to her for a long time before putting her down. His strong hand released its grip on her; the iron bars that were his fingers pulled back and gave her body freedom.

"I WILL RETURN TO DECIDE YOUR FATE."

Goliath plodded back to the front lines to mock the Israelites.

Wren stretched out her arms and legs to work out the cramps. At least she was free from the giant's clutches.

But the freedom didn't last long. Two new soldiers appeared and dragged her back to the tent. They pushed her inside, and she wondered what was going to happen next.

Time passed and pushed the sun below the horizon.

The temperature fell and chilled Wren, forcing her to sit in the middle of the tent with her knees pulled up to her chest. A growing wind rustled the tent flaps.

Then she smelled smoke. She peered out from an opening in the tent and saw some Philistine soldiers sitting around a campfire. They were talking, but she couldn't understand what they were saying. It looked like they were pointing back at something, but the absence of light made it hard for her to see.

As she brought her eyes back to the fire, she saw a lady standing there. The lady looked like her new friend Josephine! Josephine stood and stared at the fire. The logs shifted, sending a shower of sparks upward into the dark night like orange fireflies drifting in different directions.

A handful of the fire sparks floated up over the soldiers and landed on Wren's tent. The orange embers burned holes in the fabric and landed on the ground inside the tent. Another shower of sparks rose up over the fire and again floated over and landed on her temporary cell. These new embers were larger than the first and not only burned holes in the fabric but also caught the material on fire.

Wren hurried out of the tent expecting to run into a soldier.

But there was no one in sight. She saw a whole section of tents on fire just off to her left. As the flames reached higher into the night sky, a black and yellow butterfly danced away from the fire. The beautiful creature flitted through the dark night and landed on Wren's arm. A tiny pulse echoed over her skin, coming from the delicate insect as a greeting. Its sheer wings opened and closed, gently, to the slow rhythm of some unheard tune.

How did a butterfly survive the fire?

She looked but couldn't find Josephine. She did see the Israelites camped on the far side of the valley. That's where she had to go, but the giant and the army stood between her and them.

She had to do something. The butterfly took flight and disappeared behind the burning tents. Wren followed it as she slipped through the shadows and eventually made her way toward the perimeter of the Philistine camp, careful not to been seen.

A man emerged from the darkness. He wasn't dressed

like the other Philistine soldiers. He moved toward Wren at a quick pace. She took up a fighter's stance, hands clenched in fists raised together just below her face. Left foot forward. Right foot back. Torso turned so that her left side faced the stranger.

"It's me," the newcomer said.

Wren couldn't make out the man's face. "David?"

"Wren, yes, it's me. David!"

The two new friends stealthily made their way to the edge of the camp and looked out on the wide-open valley before them.

"There!" Voices behind them shouted in anger.

Wren looked back and saw a group soldiers pointing at her and David.

They had been spotted.

Where was Josephine? It would be awesome if they could do that flying trick again to escape and land safely back in the Israelite camp.

But the Philistine soldiers were running down the hill now in close pursuit.

And behind them rose another cloud of dark shadows. The swirling bands of black smoke shattered into many pieces. The pieces morphed into the human-looking figures she'd seen earlier.

The horde of soldiers, both men and dark shadows, came after them like rain after thunder and lightning.

David ran.

And Wren ran after him.

Like her life depended on it.

CHAPTER 11

She ran so hard her leg muscles felt like they were about to explode.

David kept getting out in front of her in the race to escape the Philistines and the army of shadows. He tried to stop a few times to check on her, but she continued to wave him on toward the Israelite camp.

As she ran behind David, praying that they'd make it without getting hurt, an invisible hand lifted her off the ground, and she started flying again. But this time she was not riding on the back of Josephine.

The wind rushed past her face, and the ground fell away like she was a plane taking off, leaving the airport far behind.

"David!" Wren yelled, but her friend couldn't hear

her. She was too far up in the air now.

Down below, he turned around and looked for her. He finally saw Wren and waved, but the soldiers and the dark shadows were almost upon him, so he took off running again toward the camp.

The world spun around in circles as Wren's body did a few barrel rolls high above the earth. Her stomach was having a hard time keeping up with all the changes in motion. When she leveled out, she felt like she was on a roller coaster that was suspended from the tracks.

She looked down and saw a band of light wrapped around her waist.

Now she was over the Israelite camp, soaring in a figure eight. That's when she saw David safely reach the camp too.

A wall of glittering, crystalline shapes rose up in front of the Israelites. Wren didn't know how this flying thing worked, but she wanted to get closer to see what was happening. She also wanted to meet back up with David and tell him about this flying stuff!

Descending, she could see that the shapes had

delicate blue-colored wings and emitted shards of brilliant light. And getting closer still, she saw they were actually butterflies!

The human-like shadows that had been in pursuit of David broke into a thousand pieces of black. In no time, the pieces took flight as dark birds and soared straight into the butterflies. The birds tried attacking the butterflies, but when the tiny creatures were hit, they just turned into flashes of light.

When Wren looked back where the Israelites had been, beyond the wall of butterflies, all she saw was a pasture filled with sheep. The peaceful creatures had their heads down, grazing, completely unaware of the bizarre battle being waged around them. This vision made her feel like God was showing her how He takes care of His people. In this new place, the battlefield was gone. . . .

One of the birds, its wings spread wide like a hungry hawk scouring the sky for prey, left the others and zeroed in on Wren. The creature closed the distance between them in seconds. Wren tried to dive and change directions, but it was useless, because the hawk was the more skilled of the two.

It stretched out its talons and snagged her shirt. The band of light that had been around her waist snapped away and gravity took over.

Speeding toward the valley far below, Wren prayed desperately.

The hawk swooped down and snatched her body up before she hit the ground. Even though she was much heavier than the bird, she couldn't escape its supernatural grip.

Other hawks, all black with bloodred eyes, circled in the air around her.

The raptor carried Wren back to the cliff where Mark Grant had protected her. She was dropped and fell down on the hard earth.

A stab of pain ran up her right leg. When she looked around the predator was gone.

The dark man, Ra'zeil stood before her.

How did he get here?

How could that bird carry me like that?

"I don't know who you are, but I do know you're special. The angels watch over you." Ra'zeil stepped closer with each word that came from his shadowy lips.

Wren looked around for Josephine.

"All you need to do is help me."

The smoky clouds roiled beneath the demon's translucent skin. He shut his eyes for the longest time. She blinked and then jumped. It looked like her mother was now standing there in front of her. Close enough to touch! How did her mother get here?

"Mommy?"

But when she blinked again, her mother had disappeared, and the shadow man was back in front of her.

"No, I'm not Mommy. But I can tell you where to find her."

Wren was confused. How did this thing in front of her know about her mother?

"Let's go. We don't have much time."

She was exhausted.

Where was her father?

How could she leave this crazy place and get back to him?

"Are you ready to help me?"

Wren's eyes filled with tears. She was at the breaking point. There was only so much she could take.

There was no way out.

But she knew that whatever this thing was, it wasn't good. Helping it was not an option.

"No."

Ra'zeil looked at her, his mesmerizing eyes swirls of red and gray. "Are you sure? I am the one in charge here. The giant will do as I command. If you help me, I will make sure you get home in one piece."

Goliath lumbered over to where they were standing.

Home. She wanted to be home more than anything. The creature's words were inviting. She wanted to see her dad and feel his strong arms around her. Yes, home sounded perfect now.

Goliath reached out his hand to grab her.

"Last chance, Wren Evans. You will either help me, or you will suffer in the giant's hand."

That's when she saw the neon-green card sticking out of her jeans pocket.

With God, anything.

Wren had to believe that God meant what He said and that He was a keeper of promises.

God, please help me get out of here!

"No, I will not help you. My God will save me."

CHAPTER 12

Goliath snatched Wren up off the rocky ground and held her high in the air for the whole Philistine army to see. He yanked her up so hard and fast she thought she was going to pass out.

Despite the way the Bible story ended, she was not going to be as lucky as the young shepherd boy.

Her luck had finally run out.

She writhed in the giant's powerful grip like a snake, trying to break free, but it was no use. She was a fourth-grader, and he was a nine-foot-tall superhuman.

The giant squeezed his fist and slowly pushed the air from Wren's lungs.

As she hung there, high above the plain, her life slipped away.

"They are sending a boy to battle you!"

Her lungs were squeezing shut in Goliath's hand. But her mind was still crystal clear.

The boy was David, and he was going to get rid of the nasty giant with a sling and a stone!

All she had to do was hold on a little while longer.

"AM I A DOG, THAT YOU COME AT ME WITH STICKS?"

The giant's deep voice boomed like a bomb going off in Wren's brain. She was slipping away, unable to hold on to life.

"COME HERE, AND I'LL GIVE YOUR FLESH TO THE BIRDS AND THE WILD ANIMALS!"

She thought about her poor father crying in the rain. If she died out here in the giant's hand, that would be the end of him. First her mother and now her.

He would be devastated.

She heard a softer voice this time. It sounded familiar but very far away.

"I come against you in the name of the Lord Almighty, the God whom you have defied!"

David! Yes, it was David!

"This day the Lord will deliver you into my hands!"

She tried one last time to fight back against the beast of a man. She pushed against his clenched fist with everything she had.

The world grew dim and her vision blurred.

The end was almost here.

As she hung high above the land, Wren could barely make out the shape of the shepherd approaching. Her brain was foggy from fright and pain.

Wren tried calling David's name, but she didn't have anything left. She saw David raise his arm to the giant.

Was he going to sling the stone that would take Goliath down?

The card in my pocket. The green index card!

The thought was a long shot, but it was all she had.

Lord, please help me!

Wren summoned all her strength and managed to reach a hand into her jeans pocket. She felt the index card and pulled it out.

Please, God!

Goliath's attention was on David. She could see her friend reach into a bag and pull out a stone.

She used both hands to roll the card into a tight tube.

"Hey!" Wren yelled to her captor.

The giant pulled her closer to him.

She could see David now holding the sling.

Wren shoved the index card into the giant's left eye, and his grip loosened on her. She bit hard into Goliath's thumb, and his hand opened farther.

He let go of her, and she thought she would be free, but the giant scrambled and caught her right shoe. Wren hung in the air, upside down.

Please, God! Help me!

Wren used her left foot to push her right shoe off.

The shoe inched off her heel. . . .

The blood rushed to her head. . . .

It was getting harder to concentrate. . . .

Sweat from the struggle filled her eyes.

Wren used her last ounce of strength to push. . .

. . .push. . .push on the shoe.

It popped off!

As she fell, Wren saw David's stone slam deep into the giant's forehead.

She hit the ground, and her body exploded in pain.

The massive superhuman fell facedown onto the ground, inches away from her.

David won! He killed the giant just like the Bible said he did!

As she lay there on the ancient field, unable to move, Wren wished she could at least see her father.

But her body was broken, and there was no going back.

The end was here, and the darkness was coming.

Fast.

CHAPTER 13

PRESENT DAY

MULVANE, KANSAS

Wren opened her eyes. She was still on the sidewalk holding the green index card.

She took a deep breath.

She was alive!

Not in the past, but right here, right now, in the present.

She exhaled slowly.

That's when she noticed her dad. He was on his hands and knees in the middle of the street. Red lights swirled around her new world like the misty arms of an alien who had come to take her and her father to another world.

Then the painful memory came back like a tidal wave. First the bus turning on her street. Then the fire engines.

Wren took another deep breath and wiped her face. She exhaled once more and stood up. She reread the verse on the index card:

"With man this is impossible, but with God all things are possible."

Somehow, in some weird way, she now understood the truth of those words. She knew it was true. With God's help she had just fought a giant. Wren had witnessed David take the giant's life with a sling and a stone.

She put the card in her pocket and ran back down the street, not a broken, hopeless child, but something different. Someone changed.

She ran to her father. God had given her the faith to see things in a whole new way. If young David could stand up to the mighty giant named Goliath, then she could rely on God to get through the "giant" of her mother being gone and their house destroyed. And whatever else might happen in the future.

"Dad!"

Her father took his hands from his tear-stained face and looked at his daughter. "Wren. I'm so sorry, baby. I can't believe this. I cannot believe this junk keeps happening to us."

She thought back to what she saw in the Valley of Elah. The Israelite army looked at the problem called Goliath and cowered in fear. But David showed up with a totally different attitude.

David showed up with God.

David thought about God, and not the outcome.

All David cared about was stopping the giant from mocking God.

The whole Bible experience made Wren realize that she shouldn't focus on the problems, but she should focus on God. Period. End of discussion.

Just God.

"Dad, don't say you're sorry. This stuff is just stuff. We've got this."

Her father considered his daughter's words and

looked at her like she was someone else. He shook his head and gave her a hug.

"I'm so sorry about your book," he said.

"Dad, what did I just tell you? Stop saying you're sorry." Wren remembered being in the giant's steel grip and looking down at David with just his sling and the stones. She remembered finding peace in the fact that God was in charge of the outcome!

"I just feel terrible, sweetheart. All these bad things keep happening to us, and I feel helpless."

"Trust me," she said. "Let's start following God's lead. Believe me, He knows what He's doing."

Her father was speechless. He looked at Wren like her face was covered in some horrible skin disease.

"I mean it. It's time we start becoming *followers*."

Wren stood up and helped her dad do the same. She took his hand and led him to his truck.

A handful of neighbors came over and offered their homes if they needed a place to stay. They offered money and food too. It was all very generous, but Wren whispered something in her dad's ear. He nodded and quickly helped her get into the truck's passenger seat. He jogged back around and hopped in behind the wheel. They shut the doors.

"Dad, things are going to be a lot different now."

"I know, baby. The house and—"

Wren turned to face her father. "No, Dad. I'm not talking about the house. I'm talking about *us*!"

Her dad shook his head and rubbed his face. He turned in his seat to face her. "I don't understand. What's happened to you?"

"You can't imagine! Now, come on. Let's go take Mom a flower."

ooooo

The Eternal Rest Cemetery spread out before her like an unwanted, uninvited dream. Going there would never get easier.

Tiny roads branched off the main drive like little black rivers leading cars of people to places where questions never get answered. To places where grave markers display names and dates and maybe an angel or two and perhaps even a cross.

Wren hated it, but she had no choice. She would go because she knew how much it helped her dad to have her there beside him.

"Thank you, honey. Thank you for coming with me."

"Sure, Dad. We've got this." She heard the optimism in her voice and was surprised.

Wren's father pulled the truck to the edge of the road and stopped. He sat there with the engine running for a while. The time behind the wheel, waiting to get out, shortened with each visit.

Life was not the same—never would be the same—without her mother in it.

She took another deep breath and exhaled.

They got out and made their way through the grave markers.

So many lives.

So many stories.

After a few minutes, they stopped in front of the one they came for.

RACHEL EVANS
Beautiful Mother and Wife
1980–2018

Wren grabbed her dad's hand. "We forgot the flower."

"Quite frankly, I don't think your mother cares."

They both laughed, and, strangely, it felt good.

After a while of standing in silence, Wren started talking out loud. "Well, Mom, the house just burned down. Other than that, we're good."

Wren looked at her dad, and they both burst out laughing again.

Minutes passed, and she looked around the cemetery.

So many people who left loved ones behind.

So many souls. . .

"Hey, Wren, can I ask you something?"

"Sure. What's up?"

Her dad let go of her hand and rubbed his face. "I saw a butterfly."

Wren didn't get it. Butterflies were a common sight in their little corner of the world.

"In the flames. When I was staring at the house burning, I saw a butterfly right in the middle of the fire. Am I losing my mind?"

Hearing her father talk about losing his mind brought the whole David and Goliath experience back. "Dad, uh, no, I don't think you're going crazy. What did it look like?"

"Well, it was this brilliant yellow and black color. Beautiful creature in the middle of the disaster. How on earth did the thing survive the fire?"

That's when the memory came back to her. She had seen a similar yellow and black butterfly! When she was trapped in the Philistine camp. Some of the soldiers had started a fire nearby, and from where she was being held, Wren could see the butterfly. It looked like the thing was dancing in the flames. Just like what her dad was describing.

"I don't know, but I'll tell you something crazy if you promise not to laugh at me."

"Promise."

She proceeded to relay her *experience* and ended with seeing the same type of butterfly as he saw. She thought about the lessons and the hard truths that still remained here in the real world.

David had trusted God and stood up to Goliath. In

the end, good conquered evil. But here in the garden of graves, it felt to Wren as though death had won. Her mother was gone, and the concrete cross testified that she wasn't coming back.

No sooner than she had that thought, a beautiful butterfly came into view. Its delicate wings were painted bright lemon yellow and framed in black. The graceful creature seemed to dance on the air in front of them.

This could not be real. The cemetery. Her dad. The butterfly. Wren shut her eyes and expected to see David and the giant. She felt lightheaded. No, this could not be happening.

But it was!

"Wren, do you see it?" Her dad pointed to the graceful creature that had just landed on her mother's headstone.

"Yes! I cannot believe it!"

Both father and daughter stood still looking at the butterfly. They didn't want it to ever fly away.

"It's like God is telling us that everything is going to be okay." Wren's dad hugged her as he said the same words she had in her head.

"Dad, I still can't believe this."

"I know, baby. I don't get it."

When they finally said goodbye and headed back to the truck, the butterfly took flight and danced across the air. It seemed to follow them for a few paces, then it pumped its wings and managed to get out in front of Wren and her father.

"There he goes," Wren announced.

They watched the butterfly land on a cardboard box in the bed of the truck. Wren put her hand out, palm up, next to it. The butterfly walked from the box to her hand, its tiny legs tickling her skin as it moved.

"That's weird."

"What?" Wren was still transfixed by the butterfly in her hand.

"Well, I don't remember putting that box in the truck."

"No?"

"No. Maybe one of the firefighters stuck it in there. I don't know."

"Probably," she said. "You were really out of it, you

know, like in shock when I got off the bus."

When her dad headed for the driver's seat, the butterfly took off from Wren's hand and landed back on the box.

"Do you know what's in it?" she asked.

"No idea. Let's see." He lowered the tailgate, reached in, and pulled the box to the edge of the bed. The butterfly stayed on the box.

Wren watched as her dad lifted the flaps.

No way!

She and her dad just stared at each other in shock.

The butterfly took flight and danced in the air over the box before flying away. . .up over the roof and out of sight.

"I don't believe it."

Wren shook her head. "Me neither."

There in the box was her complete manuscript! Saved from the fire. Ready to be mailed to the publisher.

"How did that get there?"

"I don't know." She pulled the notecard out of her pocket and waved it. "But looking at my book in that box helps me believe that God is a lot more powerful than I give Him credit for."

"Yes, sweetheart. You've got that right. Come on. Let's go see if we can find ourselves a place to live."

CHAPTER 14

THIRTY-THREE WEEKS LATER

The published book that honored her mother and other people who battled cancer didn't take away all of life's problems, but it did give Wren hope.

Some days were better than others. It was fun when her publisher forwarded emails from readers who wrote how *Possible* gave them hope in the middle of the darkness. Other days were filled with the grim reality that her mother was gone. The mixture of joy and sadness that defined Wren's days was becoming her new normal.

Her daydreams made her forget that she had come to the park to walk her dog this morning. The tugging of the leash brought her back to the moment.

"Come on, Makki!" Wren's chocolate-colored Shih

Tzu was trying to make his way over to a bench where a lady and a little girl were sitting. The woman had a picture book in her hand, and the little girl had something green in hers.

"I'm sorry," Wren said. "He just loves people."

"He's beautiful. I was just reading a story to my daughter about a puppy who loves peanut butter."

Wren gave a polite smile but quickly noticed a second book on the bench between the mother and the girl.

No way!

"Did you read that one yet?" she asked, pointing to the book on the bench.

"This?" The mother picked up the book and held it out for Wren.

"Yes," she said. She took the book, and it felt like a warm hug. The kind of hug that her mother gave.

"It's so cool. A girl wrote this to honor her mother who passed away from cancer. Well, that's not cool, but the cool part is that all the money from the book sales goes right to cancer research."

"That *is* cool." Wren flipped through the pages, never

once getting used to the fact that her and Beth's hard work had actually gotten published. Even all these months later, it was still a blessing to see the finished book.

The mother seemed ready to keep talking, but Wren needed to go. It was hard, because she missed her mother. Talking to this mother, or any mother for that matter, made Wren wish she could talk to her own mother. No amount of time would fill the hole her mother's passing had made in her heart. "Thanks. Come on, Makki."

She started walking away then heard the little girl's voice.

"Butterfly!"

Wren stopped and turned back. The little girl was pointing to a page in her book.

"Look. A butterfly!"

The girl's mother apologized. "I'm sorry. Emma here just loves butterflies."

"That's okay. I love butterflies too!" But what Wren didn't say was that there wasn't a butterfly in the book. She and Beth had talked about putting some in, but they didn't.

Wren looked at where the little girl was pointing and

couldn't believe it. Right there in front of her—in her book—was a yellow and black butterfly!

"Where did you get this book? Amazon?"

The mother sensed the concern in Wren's voice. "Is something wrong?"

She didn't want to share the truth, because the lady wouldn't understand. She would think Wren was crazy. "No. I just. . .my mom died of cancer, and I think this book is really cool."

The mother stood. "I am so sorry. My friend at church, Josephine, gave us the book. My sister—Emma's aunt—lost her battle with cancer last month."

"I'm sorry too. Well, I guess I should be going. It was really nice to meet you guys."

"It was nice meeting you."

Josephine?

Wren and her father had found a small two-bedroom apartment that overlooked the park. Wren saw her dad on the deck waving at her. She waved back. As she got closer to the apartment, she could tell that her father was not really waving *at* her but waving her to hurry up.

She picked up Makki and jogged the rest of the way back.

"Hey, what's up?"

Her father had a you're-not-going-to-believe-this look on his face. "I got an email from the publisher of your book. They forwarded me a really cool note from a lady named Josephine."

"Who?" First the lady in the park and now her dad.

"It's from someone here in Mulvane named Josephine. She says that she's proud of you and that God is using you to do great things for His kingdom. That *Possible* is just the beginning."

Josephine.

Josephine had to be the same lady from the Goliath adventure. Josephine was not a common name like Mary or Sarah.

Wren found her cell phone and called Beth. Her friend answered on the third ring.

"What's up?"

"Beth, I need you to check your copies of *Possible* and tell me if there's a yellow and black butterfly on page three."

"Are you okay?"

"Yes, I'm fine. Just check page three."

"Wren, we didn't put a butterfly in the book. You know that."

"I know," Wren said. "I know. Please just go check."

"Fine, I'll check. Hold on."

She stared at her father while she waited for Beth to get back.

What is going on?

"Wren?"

"Yes, Beth. What did you find?"

"Sorry, sister. No butterflies. I checked all of my copies. None."

"Thanks, Beth. Text me."

"Will do."

She hung up and went out on their apartment's deck. They had a great view of the park. She looked over to the bench where the mother and little girl had been. In their place sat a lady with a stack of books in her hands. Although Wren wasn't certain, she wondered if the books were hers.

"Dad, come with me."

"Where are we going?"

"The park."

"Weren't you just there?"

"Yes. Come on."

This time Makki stayed behind. Wren gave her dog a bear hug and told him they would be right back. The furry little guy whimpered, *Hurry up!*

When they got to the bench, she saw that the lady was holding a stack of *Possible* books. The lady looked very familiar.

"Hello."

"Hi, friend."

"I'm Wren, and this is my dad."

"I know. My name's Josephine."

"Josephine?"

"Yes, dear. It's me."

Wren saw her. The clothes were different, but this *was* the same Josephine from the Goliath adventure!

"Where did you get those books?" She pointed to the stack Josephine was still holding on to.

"Well, that's really not important right now. The dragon is coming! Stars will fall!"

Wren started to turn back to her father and tell him who Josephine was.

"Open their eyes that they may see!"

Wren and her father turned back, and the woman was no longer alone on the bench. A man wearing a blue button-down dress shirt and jeans sat next to Josephine. And behind them stood more people. Behind the group of men and women who were standing, Wren saw a row of at least ten beautiful horses, all different in color. There appeared to be ten fires burning behind the horses.

"Whoa!" Wren grabbed her dad's hand. "What is that?"

"I don't know, but come on, honey, let's get out of here!" Her dad sounded like he was done. "I don't know what this is, but it's not safe."

"Wren, I think you know Mark. And these are our friends." Josephine waved a hand above her head to indicate the people and the horses waiting behind her. The people waved at Wren and her father.

"Hold on, Dad." She watched Josephine a little longer.

"Wren, I told your dad in the email that this book is just the beginning. There's a massive war coming, and you can help stand up to the enemy. There are more children just like you who have been back to the Bible times. All of you will serve a beautiful purpose in the battle."

Josephine rattled off the names of the specific children and the stories they had experienced.

"Come on, Wren. These people are crazy. Now!" Her dad grabbed her by the hand and started pulling her away from the bench.

As they turned to head back to the apartment, a massive cloud of yellow and black butterflies danced in the air. The delicate creatures moved over them and around them. Wren felt a surge of joy go through her body as she felt the flutter of wings move across her skin.

When the butterflies all scattered on the wind, her dad looked at her. "What's happening to us?"

"I don't know, but I don't feel afraid." She looked back over her shoulder. The horses, the people that were standing, and all the fire had vanished. Just the man named Mark and the lady Josephine remained. They were still sitting on the park bench.

"Wren!"

It was Josephine.

Wren turned back. "Yes."

"You're not alone. In fact, you are never alone and never will be alone. You are loved more than you will ever know."

She looked at her dad again. "This *is* crazy."

"Yes, baby, it is. But after that wave of butterflies came over us, I don't feel afraid either. Wanna go sit with them and hear what they have to say?"

"Sure, Dad. Love you."

He gave Wren a huge bear hug. "Love you too, angel."

Wren and her dad made their way back to the bench and sat down, in between Josephine and Mark. The four of them talked until the sun was way long gone.

By the time they got up to head back to their apartment, Wren had more questions than answers.

They said their goodbyes, and Josephine promised that the four of them would see one another again very soon.

Wren had seen God work in mighty ways.

A giant had fallen.

Somehow the unseen had become visible.

And, most of all, despite her mother passing and the house burning, her heart felt full again. That was the biggest act of grace God had shown her since all the bad things started happening.

When they got back to the apartment, Wren found the green note card with the Bible verse her mother had written out. She took it out onto the deck. She reread it with new eyes. Given everything she had just experienced, God had become bigger. He really was bigger than the hard times.

"Thank You, God."

Wren held up the card toward the starry night sky and waved it back and forth. It was her very small way of celebrating her Creator.

"Thank You!"

Her dad came out and joined her. "You okay?"

"Yep. How 'bout you?"

"I'm good."

Wren thought for a second and held the green card up for her dad to see. "Now what?"

"Well, Josephine said a lot of crazy things, but you got to experience David and Goliath! I think we find the other kids she was talking about and go from there."

Wren thought about all the things Josephine and Mark had told them. There were other kids out there who had gotten to relive Bible stories. The boy from Texas, Corey, went back to the time of Noah. Kai, a girl from Florida, relived the ten plagues and met Moses. And then there was Jake, a boy from North Carolina who had been able to see ancient Jericho.

"Yes, Dad, let's do it!"

They held hands and looked back up at the stars. It felt really good to be part of a team. And it felt good to feel loved, despite the losses in life. But most of all, it felt good knowing that God was in charge.

Of everything.

ABOUT THE AUTHOR

Matt Koceich is a husband, father, and public school-teacher. Matt and his family live in Texas.